# NIGHT
# OF THE
# LIVING
# INFLATABLE
# LOVEDOLLS

Don't touch!

ISBN: 978-0-9839069-8-8

Cover Concept, Artwork and Design: J.H. Glaze
Text Editing: Susan Grimm

First Printing May 2014
Published by MostCool Media Inc.
"Make it interesting. Make it MostCool."

Proudly printed in the United States of America.

First Edition May 2014

10 9 8 7 6 5 4 3 2 1

# NIGHT
# OF THE
# LIVING
# INFLATABLE
# LOVEDOLLS

## J. H. GLAZE

# ONE

The heat rose from the surface of the two-lane highway in waves that warped the landscape into a mirage of shimmering wet pavement and undulating grasses. To the lone armadillo, it was just another hot afternoon as he meandered toward the yellow lines in the middle of the road scavenging for something to eat.

Half blinded by the bright sunlight, he did not see the eighteen-wheeler barreling toward him at top speed. The roar of the giant tires and the shockwave of air and sound as it breezed past forced him to stop, paralyzed by fear. His appetite no longer in control, he tried to run, hell bent on reaching safer ground. He paid no mind to the family in the black SUV that had just reached his exact location.

Billy Joe Jackson checked the side mirror on the cab of his eighteen-wheeler as he sped away. Glad to miss the poky little armadillo, he could have sworn that the driver of the SUV had swerved to do the same. He hoped that his eyes were not playing tricks on him, preferring to blissfully drive on and never knowing for sure whether it survived. It would have dampened his day to know that the timid creature had met his fate beneath the wheels of the family's vehicle.

He took the last hit off the joint he had been smoking and tossed the remainder out the window. There was more where that came from, so there was no need to save the shorts. Besides, the smell of pot was a lot stronger after it had burnt for a while, and he really didn't need the hassle of getting pulled over for something minor and then getting hauled off for a DUI.

"Whatcha been smoking, boy?" would be the question. The fines for possession and driving under the influence would be bad enough, but losing his job because of it would really suck ass. Paranoia prompted him to check his speed once again.

There were a lot of small town cops hanging out along this road, parked on hidden side streets to nowhere. They would sit napping or tossing back donuts until some unsuspecting speeder would get snagged in their radar net. Then, they would come scurrying out like a fat spider having just discovered a fat grasshopper thrashing about in their web.

Billy Joe didn't need any of that. Not today. He slowed the rig down to just two miles over the speed limit. *That should be good enough for any backwater deputy.* At least, he hoped that would be the case. He was on his way to pick up the second half of his load for the day and wanted to be on time.

About a hundred and twenty miles back, he had made the first pick up at the Imperial Leisure Imports warehouse. Earlier that morning, he had wondered why everybody at the depot was snickering and cutting up about his haul for the day. The boss laughed so hard when he handed Billy Joe the clipboard with the assignment that his last slurp of coffee had come blowing out his nose. At the time, the trucker did not get the joke.

It turned out that Imperial Leisure Imports was a major distributor for sex toys or as they called them, *leisure products*, hence the company name. Billy Joe and his friends just called them dildos, vibrators, and blow-up fuck dolls. He could not see the logic of working up a fancy name for them. After all, he was an old-school trucker. He had made his fair share of "rest" stops at the roadside strip clubs and adult bookstores located just off the highway. They were always tucked away in the middle of some last chance bumfuck town, selling any and every type of sex toy and low budget porn flick imaginable.

3

Every trucker, well, most of them anyway, knew what it was like to run the gauntlet of pocket pussies and penis lube. It was the path you had to take as you made your way to the stage where some of the homeliest strippers that ever graced a lap dance devoted themselves to twelve-hour shifts just to feed two kids and a cat. Funny thing was, after a straight ten-hour haul, those *girls* were just what a burned out trucker needed in order to unwind. He and so many others in his profession were grateful for that seductive wink, that special smile, even if it *was* missing a tooth or two.

He was smiling as he drove off to his next destination. He was now hauling a massive load of jiggles and giggles in his trailer and, in about a half hour, he would arrive at the second stop of this run. Thanks to his former military service and a cousin who worked at the Pentagon, he had managed to obtain the security clearance necessary for his second and last pickup of the day.

Fort Rogers was the Army's foremost research facility in all of the fifty states. He was not sure what he would be hauling out of there, but he didn't care. Any run for the government paid twice as much as a regular load, and he needed the cash for the down payment on his new Harley Iron, which had to be damn near the most beautiful thing he had ever seen and he had to have it, no matter the sacrifice to get it.

Billy Joe was feeling good. For about the last fifty miles or so, he had *Lynrd Skynrd* playing in his head, and he was half singing, half mumbling *Sweet Home Alabama*. It was about time to push in the CD and listen to the song the way it was meant to be enjoyed.

# TWO

At Fort Rogers, the mood on the loading dock was somber. It was late afternoon, and the soldiers came and went with a sense of urgency that lacked even a hint of lighthearted banter. Those on the dock finished strapping the four fifty-gallon drums to the wooden pallet while Billy Joe waited. He observed that there were a lot more warning stickers on them than ones he had picked up in the past. When he tried to move in closer to read what was written on them, an armed MP stepped into his path.

"I'm sorry, sir, but you're going to have to step back." He pointed the barrel of his rifle in Billy Joe's direction, his finger resting uncomfortably on the trigger

No need to be told twice, especially by a gun-toting soldier. He walked back to the cab of the truck and waited while the pallet was loaded into his trailer. He heard some shouting at one point, and he felt the trailer rock a bit. He guessed that the forklift driver had brushed the load against the wall, and he hoped there was no damage. If that were the case, the haul might not be so profitable after all.

His mind was left to all kinds of imaginings since he wasn't permitted to watch while the drums were loaded. It would be futile to confront anyone here with questions, so he settled back in the seat and closed his eyes. He was just drifting off to sleep when someone pounded on the door of the cab. Bleary eyed, Billy Joe rolled down the window.

"Yeah, what's up?"

"Your load is ready. Captain needs you to sign the papers," the stone-faced soldier replied.

By the time he was out of the cab, the soldier was gone. Billy Joe climbed the concrete steps, looking to his left to see that the doors of the trailer had been closed. A seal had been applied just above the padlock that secured the load from the thieves that frequented truck stop parking lots. The shipping officer standing on the loading dock appeared to be perturbed as he silently held out a clipboard for his signature.

"Must be haulin' some important stuff today," Billy Joe grumbled as he stared at the stack of papers on the clipboard.

"Yeah, we wouldn't want anybody to steal that load of dildos you're hauling. Geezus, man." He tossed the driver a stern look and pulled the clipboard back.

Billy's discomfort with the whole business must have shown. The soldier cracked a huge smile and roared with laughter, slapping him on the shoulder.

"I'm just bustin' yer balls. I don't give a shit what you're haulin'. Just get my barrels to the base in one piece and you'll be golden in my book. Or should I say... golden shower?" He laughed again, then held out the clipboard and pen and added with a straight face, "Read and initial the warning statements."

This was new. Billy Joe never had to read and sign off on any warning papers. Normally, there was just one sheet to sign. It all seemed serious enough, so he took the time to read each warning before initialing them.

*Toxic Substance: Do not swallow or inhale vapors.* He initialed with *BJ*.

*Corrosive Liquid: Do not allow contact with skin or eyes.* He initialed with *BJ*.

*Do not expose to open air or water.* He initialed with *BJ*.

*Any security breach or information leak by driver will result in criminal prosecution in a military court of law. Maximum sentence: Execution by hanging.*

"What the fuck? What the hell am I hauling?" The pen hovered over the paper, his hand beginning to shake.

"Ah… do you have a question?"

"Damn, right I have a question! What's this execution by hanging shit?"

"It's a new form. Don't get excited. We even use it for the laundry service." The soldier looked away, saying, "Come on, just sign the damn thing. I don't have all night!" He held out his hand for the clipboard. "Or, we can take it off the truck…"

"Okay, okay." Billy Joe hastily initialed the rest of the warnings without reading them and signed the bottom line.

"Here," he said, handing over the clipboard.

"Now, get that piece of shit truck of yours off my driveway. You're holding up my beer delivery!"

Billy Joe looked past the front of his rig and there was indeed a beer truck waiting for him to pull away from the dock. The soldier tore a yellow sheet of paper from the bottom of the stack and handed it to him. With a friendly, *"Drive safely,"* he sent him on his way.

# THREE

Country roads can be hazardous for truckers, especially at dusk. Deer, possums, and any other furry critter this side of the Mississippi seemed to love to throw itself beneath the tires of an eighteen-wheeler. Billy Joe tried to figure out the road-kill phenomenon one night after downing a twelve-pack with his friend Carlos. After hours of slurred speech and argumentation, followed by a momentary session of Carlos' projectile vomiting, they finally agreed on principle that it was probably the only effective way that animals could commit suicide.

Sure, a rabbit could put itself out there for a fox, but it would be a slow and painful death. Whereas, the quick crushing *Tha-thunk* of the tractor-trailer tires meant an instant release into the great beyond. The discussion with Carlos reared its ugly head once again, as the bloody smear of a young deer lying on the side of the road with its tongue hanging out passed under his wheels.

"Yet another sad soul of nature has gone to be with Jesus," Billy said aloud, doing his best to make the motions of the Catholic cross over his heart.

It was during this action of sympathy that his hand bumped the steering wheel and knocked the joint from his yellowed fingers. It fell straight into his lap. He reached for it just as it rolled from the top of his thigh and onto the seat, disappearing under his crotch. Instinctively, his ass rose from the seat as he searched for the burning ember somewhere beneath it.

He failed to realize that the truck was coming up on a curve in the road. Steering straight ahead, as he groped for the joint, he was running off the pavement. The cab began to rock, and he looked up, trying to regain control. He was nearly standing on the brake pedal when the truck slammed into a tree, shearing it off at bumper height and effectively stopping the forward momentum of the truck.

"Fuck! Fucking, fuck!" Billy Joe yelled with one hand holding his head where it had struck the windshield and the other pounding on the steering wheel. Blood began to trickle down between his fingers, and he reached for the baseball cap lying on the seat next to him. He placed it on his head and pulled the brim down to cover the injury hoping it would stop the bleeding.

\*\*\*

About a hundred yards away, a green pickup truck sat partially hidden in the woods on an old dirt road. On the wide seat, two disheveled teenagers were locked in an embrace so tight it would have required a crowbar to break them apart. Suddenly, they disengaged at the terrifying sound of the crashing tractor-trailer.

"What was that?" The girl's lips pulled away from the pimple-faced boy.

"Must have been the wind." He leaned forward again trying to resume his maneuvers.

Distracted, she pushed his face away. "The wind doesn't make a sound like *boom-crack*. I think there was an explosion somewhere over by the highway."

"Maybe it was lightning," he replied. "It's been cloudy all day."

"No, it was *not* lightning, Tucker Peters, and thunder doesn't sound like metal crashing. I think we should investigate."

"Come on, Lana. We can check it out later on the way home. Besides, what if it *was* a crash? What if it was a UFO or something? You sure you want to run into aliens right now with your shirt all unbuttoned?" He grinned as he tried to peek down her shirt.

Lana clutched her blouse and began to button it up. "How did you... I didn't even feel you..."

"Fingers of fury, just like Bruce Lee." Grinning, he held up his hand and wiggled his fingers. "Besides, it sure seemed like you *knew* I was doin' that. You didn't say nothing."

"I didn't say anything because I didn't know you were doing it. You're lucky I didn't scream or... or something." She grinned back at him and suddenly he knew that she knew exactly what he had been doing.

She slid closer to him and purred, "Come on, Tuck, please? I really want to find out what it was. Somebody might need our help."

Looking into her green eyes, he felt a rush of hormones pumping into his bloodstream. "Alright, okay, but I don't wanna just go racing out there. The highway patrol might already be poking around. We'll just get close enough to see from the woods."

He slid behind the wheel and turned the key. With the truck in gear, they crept down the dirt road toward the highway.

"I bet it's nothing anyway."

\*\*\*

Billy Joe was standing at the back of the truck looking at the seal on the door. He would need some kind of tool to cut it off before he could check the load inside. The paperwork he had signed stated specifically that he should call an 800 number immediately if anything happened to the load. How was he supposed to tell if something had happened if he didn't open the doors and look? He figured if the load was undamaged, he could call a tow truck and get his rig back on the road.

He had already inspected the front of the truck, and it looked fine, except for the dirt clods and grass stuck in the wheels and steering assembly. He went back to the cab and grabbed a hammer and a flashlight from a toolbox under his seat. He would pop the seal, look in the truck, check the cargo and close the door. No big deal. Later, he would explain it by saying he had gotten run off the road by a drunk driver. It happened often on these back roads and would be a totally believable story.

Walking back along the trailer, he heard a thumping sound coming from inside. It was faint, but he was certain there was something inside the trailer making the sound. Could someone be in there? He knew there had been no one in there when he left the Imperial Leisure Imports warehouse. He had personally checked the load to ensure that it was tied down securely. However, he had been kept from getting near the trailer before they sealed it at the base.

Could there have been a soldier inside assigned to ride with the drums? What if someone was injured in the crash? Billy Joe's mind was spinning with thoughts of what might happen if a soldier had been injured. It would definitely be the end of his fat government checks. Standing next to the trailer, he called out to whomever might be locked up inside.

"Hello. Is anybody in there? Are you hurt?"

There was no response, except for a continuous thumping from within. He stepped to the back of the rig with a heightened sense of urgency and began pounding on the seals that were wrapped through the holes in the dual door handles.

"I'm getting this thing opened. Hang in there, buddy." He tried to be reassuring, though he was still not sure if someone was in there.

\*\*\*

From behind a stand of pine trees, Tucker and Lana watched as the driver pounded on the doors. "I told you it was a wreck," she whispered.

"And I told you it probably wasn't any big deal. He doesn't look hurt. Look at him wailin' on that door. If he was injured, he wouldn't be able to do that."

"You said it was lightning, though I'm guessing you meant thunder."

"Geez. It sounded like it to me. Anyway, all he needs is a tow truck from the looks of it." He tried to change the subject rather than admit he was wrong. "If you're worried about it, why not use your phone and call your dad?"

"I don't have a signal out here, besides my battery is almost dead. I forgot to charge it before I left the house. Do you have a charger?"

Tucker kicked his foot through the trash on the floorboards and shrugged.

"I guess I left it in the BMW," he laughed. "How 'bout we just drive over there and ask him if he needs some help. He probably already called for a tow truck."

"Wait a second. Looks like he got the doors open."

\*\*\*

Billy Joe pulled up on the handle and swung open the first door. The intense odor that rolled out of the trailer nearly knocked him down.

"Damn! That stuff smells like rotten ass!" He held his arm up to try to cover his nose as he opened the second door. Reaching into his back pocket, he pulled out a flashlight and clicked it on. "Oh shit, I'm so screwed!"

From where he stood, it appeared that everything remained intact except the barrels. The smell was proof that something had spilled from them. He noticed a dark fluid oozing toward the back of the trailer where he was now standing. He figured the best way to tell exactly what had been damaged would be to climb up into the trailer and have a look.

Setting the light on the floor, he planted his hands and pulled himself up. He picked up the light and made his way toward the rear of the trailer. He was only a third of the way in, when he saw something moving under a stack of boxes on a pallet. As he reached to move one of the boxes to see what it was, he got some of the fluid from the drums on his hand.

It felt as though his hand had burst into flame and the heat was moving quickly up his arm. He screamed in agony as it spread, and his head was pounding as he hurried back to the opening of the trailer where he lost his balance and fell face first to the ground. Coughing and choking, he managed to stand up.

\*\*\*

"Look, something strange is happening."

Lana pointed at the trucker as he got up and began gyrating wildly. She could swear that the man was swelling up like a balloon. Wide eyed, she stood gaping as he exploded into a cloud of red mist and chunks of flesh. Bits of shredded clothes hung from his exposed skeleton before it all collapsed to the ground.

At the same time, Tucker was trying to make sense of things and stood speechless while he watched the scene play out. When the remains of the driver hit the ground, he stuttered, "H-holy fuck! Wh-what the hell was that?"

"Oh, god, he exploded! What should we do?"

"I don't know. I-I think I have a tire patch kit in the back."

She punched his arm. "He exploded, Tuck! A tire patch kit is not going to put him back together. We need to get my dad."

"Shit, you know how your dad feels about me. I can't just walk into the sheriff's station, especially with you."

Considering how that had come out, he tried again. "I mean... you know what I mean."

# FOUR

Shocked at what they had witnessed, the couple sped off down the road in the pickup truck while the open trailer continued coming to life. The accident had caused two of the fifty-gallon drums to break loose, allowing them to crash into the walls of the trailer and splash a dark fluid over the dozen or so palettes of leisure products. Each palette held hundreds of boxes of sex toys. As each item came in contact with the heinous chemical, it began to swell and wriggle to life.

The resulting parade of novelty items falling from the back of the truck was the stuff of a porn actor's nightmare. Molded body parts of various shapes and sizes, quivered and shivered as they made their way to the trailer's opening and cascaded over the edge to the ground below.

One by one, the sex toys moved away from the scene, most of them pointed in the direction of Kensington, a typical, sleepy, small town where nothing ever happened...

...Until tonight.

# FIVE

The Kensington sheriff's station was being renovated, and plastic sheeting hung from the walls in several rooms to keep the dust created by the construction from permeating the rest of the building. This temporary arrangement made it necessary for the station's small staff to occupy a single large room that also served as the reception area. Since the rear exit was cordoned off, it was the only way to enter or leave the building.

On this quiet evening, only the deputy was in the office. Al Slater was manning the radio and the phone. He was dealing with anyone who needed assistance. When Tucker's pickup slid into the gravel parking lot, he stood up from his chair to see who was in such a hurry that they would be so reckless. He watched as Tucker and Lana jumped from the truck and ran to the building, bursting through the door with an air of urgency.

"Mr. Slater, where's my dad?" Lana did not bother to say hello.

Al, who was standing at the window, walked over to the teens and sized them up.

"Well, hello to you too, missy. Your dad is out on a call just now, but I think he'd be ever so interested to know…"

She cut him off. "There's a wreck out on the highway near the old Thompson Farm Road. A truck ran off the highway and hit a tree… and the driver… well, he exploded!"

She had tried to think of a way to say what she had seen without sounding crazy, but decided she might as well tell it the way that it happened. To Al, it sounded exactly as she hoped it would not.

"I'm sorry, but it sounded like you said the driver exploded," he mocked. "Maybe I misunderstood?"

She tried to be more respectful, hoping it would add credibility to her story. "No, Deputy Slater. We were watching from the dirt road in the woods. We saw him. He opened up the back of the truck and climbed up, then he fell out. He was standing there, and then it was like… *BOOM!* He was just… gone!" She was struggling to find better words to explain what she had seen.

"Really, man. I saw it, too. We heard the truck hit the tree, so we went to check it out…" Tucker tried to back up her story, but the deputy cut him off.

"Thompson Farm Road? Now what were you two doing on that abandoned road in the first place? You said you *heard* a truck hit a tree, so I'm going to take a guess… a little something we used to call parking!" He grinned and raised his eyebrows. "I'm thinkin' your dad wouldn't be too happy about that, Miss Lana."

His lack of urgency infuriated her. "Can we talk about that some other time? You need to go out there and see what happened. Find out why that guy exploded. Maybe he was hauling explosives or something."

"I can't leave the station right now. Your dad told me to stay here by the phone. But, I'll tell you what. We can give him a call and see what he has to say about it. Maybe he'll tell me to drive over there and check it out, just like you said." He turned and walked toward the desk where his radio sat silently waiting for action.

"Please don't tell him I'm with Tucker. He'll…" She realized that she might be better off not to ask such a favor at the moment.

"He'll what? Ground you? Yell at you? Maybe even spank that smart ass of yours? Yeah, I know about you and that boy there. Your dad bitches about it all the time." He

23

smiled to himself as he thought of what kind of a deal he could make with her. "This time I'll cover for you, but you're going to owe me. Big time."

Lana nodded in agreement. She had absolutely no clue what the deputy might have in mind concerning the repayment of this *debt*. Tucker, on the other hand, let his imagination run wild. He reached out and squeezed her hand.

"You need to be careful with this guy," he whispered as the deputy made the call. "He's pretty creepy. I've heard…"

Just then, the deputy put down his radio and reached for his gun. "Freeze, Peters!" he shouted, pointing his service weapon at the young man.

"What the…" Tucker took a step back.

"Step away from him, Lana. I don't want to hit you by mistake when I take down your thieving boyfriend there."

His hand shook as he pointed his weapon at Tucker.

"Your dad is out at old lady Parker's place right now. She says she saw Mr. Peters here leaving her house carrying a bag of her belongings and…" he gulped. "She says he killed her dog when he robbed her house."

"Hey, man. Just chill out." Tucker held his hands out toward the man to show he was unarmed. "I didn't break into anybody's house, and I sure as hell didn't kill Mrs. Parker's dog."

"Put your hands on the desk over there and shut up." The deputy waved his sidearm in the direction of the desk where he had dropped his radio. "You make one funny move and I'll put one in you."

As Tucker put his hands on the desk, Al fumbled with his handcuffs. He stepped behind the boy and one hand at a time slapped the cuffs on his wrists. Lana was stunned. She had been with Tucker all evening until now.

"There is no way he could have robbed that crazy old lady's house. He was with me all night."

"You just sit over there and be quiet, girlie. Your daddy is on his way here right now, and he ain't too happy. You can tell him all about it when he gets here."

He holstered his weapon and grabbed Tucker, one hand taking him by the collar of his shirt and the other holding the chain linking the handcuffs. "Meanwhile, your boyfriend here can cool his heels in a cell while we wait."

He led the boy down the hall through the plastic sheeting to the only holding cell in the station. Lana could hear the sound of the cell door closing. Her boyfriend was being locked up for a crime he had obviously not committed, and she was angry at not being able to do anything to stop it from happening.

# SIX

Miles from the sheriff's station, three young men stood in the headlights of their parked cars. They were holding several pillowcases full of items they had stolen from the old woman's house. One of them dumped the contents of his makeshift bag on the ground and stood back so the others could see the contents.

"I can't believe you killed the old lady's dog, man," one of them complained while another rifled through the stolen goods.

"Damn thing bit me. I ain't playing! That hurt like hell. Fuckin' dog was askin' for it."

The young man rubbed his arm. The dirty strip of cloth tied around it was wet with blood. "I think I'm gonna need stitches. It's bleeding like crazy."

"You shouldn't have tried to pet the damn thing. Dogs attack when they feel threatened, especially when you break into their house. Dump that bag now. We need to split this stuff up and get the fuck outta here."

The would-be leader gave the other two a shove and showed no sympathy for the injured kid. "Tomorrow, we can take this shit to the city and pawn it. Let's see what we got."

As the three boys sorted through their stolen treasures, one of them opened a wooden box. He held it up in the beam of the headlights to see what it contained.

"Holy fucking ass! Look at this."

He set the box on the ground and shoved his hand into it. When he pulled it out, he was holding a fistful of money.

"There must be a couple thousand bucks in here. We hit the jackpot this time."

"Let me see."

The other boys were jockeying to get closer when a rustling noise came from the woods. All three stopped what they were doing and looked in the direction of the sound.

"Who's out there?" the nervous leader yelled into the woods, holding his hand up to his face to block the glare of the headlights so he could see better in the darkness.

There was no verbal response, only silence.

"I think it was just the wind moving the…"

He was cut short by more sounds coming from the line of trees. It seemed to originate from more than one location.

"Shit, we're busted. Let's get the fuck out of here," the boy with the bloody rag on his arm whispered and started to move slowly toward his car before remembering the box full of money. He moved back toward his friends and into the light of the headlights.

"I don't think it's human." The leader sounded confident. "They would have come at us by now if it was people. Might be coyotes though. Find something to throw at them, just in case."

"Everything we could hit em with is over there in the woods. We got nothing except the shit we stole," the bleeder complained. "We can't take on a pack of coyotes in the dark with some candlesticks and silverware. Hell, my arm's bleeding. They can probably smell it."

He began inching toward the car again. Just then, he saw the outline of a person in the glow of the lights. It appeared to be a woman or teenage girl stumbling slowly out from behind a stand of tall grass.

"Oh shit, it's a girl."

"I can see that, but she don't look right."

The leader took a few steps forward and called to her. "Hey girl, what do you want? We were just about to leave outta here and go get us some beer. You wanna go?"

He eyed the form moving toward him. "You look like you been drinking already, the way you're walking."

The third boy had been quiet until now, but when he first saw the girl, something looked familiar about her. He just couldn't figure out what it was, and then he remembered.

"Hey, something's wrong with this deal. She don't look like she's from around here. Ain't no Japanese girls in Kensington. And she don't look like no regular girl neither. Looks like one of them life-like sex dolls they advertise on the Internet."

The leader took another step forward. "Damn, Jimmy, I think you're right. One of them ones that actually *looks* like a real girl." He pulled the baseball cap off his head and scratched. "But, how the fuck can she be walking?"

"I don't know, bro, but let's think for a minute. We know she ain't real, but you know how they say them real-like love dolls got a real-like pussy?" The boy's arm was starting to throb from the wound. He rubbed it and added, "I think we oughta check her out."

"You're right, and I got an idea."

The lead boy began to move closer to the lifelike doll. The light was dim, but he could see the painted makeup on her face. It might have been a little smeared, but she still looked better to him than most of the girls he slept with round this part of the county.

"I'm gonna grab her and get her on the ground. If she fights back, you guys grab her arms and legs. Hold her down while I fuck her. When I'm done with her, we'll switch off."

The quiet guy spoke up. "Why do you get to go first? I'm the one who figured out what she was."

The leader glared at him, "This ain't no fuckin' sheep, Jim. I doubt you even know where to find a pussy on a real girl. Now shut your trap and get ready to move."

With that, he closed in on his target. He positioned himself in front of the doll and grabbed both of its arms. As he had suspected, there was no resistance to his advance, and he felt emboldened by the erection growing in his jeans.

"Watch this!"

He leaned down to kiss the doll's cold silicone rubber lips. He was holding the doll's head as he puckered up, when a sound, something like *glorp*, came from her mouth. A black stream of projectile fluid shot from the doll and straight into his open mouth. He was trying to choke out, "*What the fuck!*" when he let out a blood curdling scream instead. The searing heat spread throughout his body and he began to swell. In an instant, he exploded.

"Oh fuck!" The kid with the bandaged arm backed away gasping as the gore from his vaporized friend sprayed over him. He stumbled as he tried to get to the car to make his escape. His skin was on fire. His eyes were blinded, and he screamed at the top of his lungs just before he exploded in a burst of red, sending his gory bits splashing over the car he was going to use for his getaway.

Jimmy stood paralyzed by fear. Fortunately, he had not been exposed to any of the fluids that had sprayed onto his friend and the car. When he finally found his legs, he sprinted back to his own car. He tripped, falling head first into a large rock and was rendered unconscious.

The love doll's momentum had slowed when its attacker had grabbed hold of it, but now it was moving on past the parked cars. It spewed its dark liquid every few feet, managing to spray the side of the car where Jimmy now lay, only a few feet from the front bumper. He was fully incapacitated.

The foul liquid dripped down the quarter panels and onto the tires. On the opposite side, the red slimy remains of the second exploding boy slid down the slick surface of the car. With an unearthly sound, the tires jerked to life and began moving independently of one another. The metal body of the car shook and rattled as the tires pressed hard against the rims.

Rolling forward toward the unconscious boy, the car advanced until a low hanging part of the frame beneath the engine caught on his shoulder. He came around when he felt the pressure of the metal dragging over his chest. He screamed for help, but there was no one around. The tires were swelling beyond their capacity and, suddenly, they exploded. The full weight of the car dropped down, crushing his chest. His open eyes faded as the life within him was extinguished.

# SEVEN

The sheriff's car pulled slowly into the parking lot of the station, its headlights lighting up the side of the building. Sherriff Wilson knew what lay ahead of him when he walked through that door, but he wasn't quite sure how he was going to handle it. He had lost track of how many times he had asked, told, scolded, yelled and begged his daughter to stay away from that Peters boy. Still, she had stubbornly ignored him, and time and again, he discovered evidence that she had been with him.

Perhaps this burglary incident would be the one thing that could send the boy to the juvenile justice center for a while. It would give Lana some time to take up an interest in something or someone else. It was possible she could recover if the object of her infatuation was unavailable for a long period. This thought gave him hope, and he quickened his step as he headed for the door.

"Your dad's here. So, you need to keep yourself quiet while I tell him what's been goin' on. I don't need no static background noise while I'm talking." The deputy was all business and was just about to threaten her with giving out other tidbits of information, when her father stepped through the door.

"Hey, Slater. What's going on around here tonight? All of a sudden trouble is whipping up like a damn tornado." Before the deputy had a chance to answer, he turned to Lana. "And what kind of trouble are *you* stirring up tonight, young lady. I heard something about your friend, who I might add you have been forbidden to see. It seems he's gotten himself into some kind of serious situation."

Against the wishes of the deputy, she blurted out, "Tucker didn't do anything, Daddy. He was with me all night, and we saw a crash over by the highway…"

"She means to say they were parking and making out over on the dirt road just off the highway." Al smirked as he twisted the knife in the girl's back. He watched the sheriff's face cycle through several shades of red.

"The old farm road?"

Sheriff Wilson was holding back the anger building up inside, unsure if this was going to ruin his plan. Although he had come to terms with the fact that his daughter disobeyed him where the Peters boy was concerned, she had never lied to him any time he ever confronted her about it. No matter how compromising the circumstance, she had always told him the truth.

"I have the kid locked up in the back, boss. I thought he was gonna make a run for it, but..."

The deputy was expecting some praise for apprehending the troublemaker. He was completely taken by surprise at what happened next.

"Please shut up, Al." He glared at his subordinate. "So, what happened out there tonight, young lady? You brought the boy here, knowing you were going to be in trouble. It must be something important."

Lana tried to gauge her father's state of mind. She couldn't quite read him at the moment, but she decided to tell him everything.

"Yes, it was important, Daddy. We were out on the dirt road, *talking*, when we heard a noise like thunder, but it wasn't. It was a big rig. He was hauling a trailer, and he'd run off the road and hit a tree."

The next part was going to be more difficult to relay, because it was going to sound crazy, but she took a breath and continued.

"After the accident, we watched the driver checking out the load on his trailer. He opened the door in the back, and… well… something happened, and he, er… exploded."

She stopped there waiting for a response.

"He exploded. Like…" Her father was looking at Slater, expecting him to start laughing. This had to be a prank. People just don't explode.

"Like he was filled with air or something, he swelled up and exploded!" She motioned with her arms to demonstrate as she spoke.

"You actually saw this? How long ago? Were there any other witnesses?"

"Yeah, Daddy, we both saw it. It was about an hour ago or more now. There wasn't any traffic on the road when it happened, so I don't think anybody else saw it."

Her father saw the look that assured him she was not making it up. Admittedly, it was a lot for any person to take in. Some guy just exploded for no apparent reason? Worse than that, his daughter had been witness to it.

"Al, go get the boy. I want to ask him some questions."

"But, Sherriff, I don't think we ought to…"

"What the fuck did I just say, Al?"

He was about to let all the pent up anger blow. He hardly ever cussed in front of his little girl.

"Yeah, okay, I'm going."

The man slinked off to the back of the building to get the boy as ordered.

"Honey, if this really happened the way you say, it might be that the trucker was hauling something dangerous, and it's still out there." He took a deep breath.

"Aside from all of that, why did you have to be out with *that* kid?" Before she could answer his question, the phone started ringing.

"Hold that thought." He pointed his index finger at her as he picked up the phone. "Sheriff's office."

A woman's voice greeted him. "Who is this?" she asked.

"Sheriff Wilson, and who is this?"

"Sorry, Sherriff. I didn't recognize the voice. It's Mrs. Parrish calling... Jimmy's mom. I'm worried about Jimmy. He was supposed to be home a couple of hours ago, but he's not here yet, and he always calls if he's going to be late. I haven't heard from him, Sheriff, and I'm worried because he left here with that scalawag captain of the football team."

"Mark Shaver?"

"Yes, that's the one. I keep telling Jimmy he's no good, what with all the stories I've heard. I just know something's wrong. Have you heard about any accidents or anything?"

"No, ma'am. Nothing like that so far tonight." He checked the desk for the call log to see what had been called in. "Tell you what, I'll be headed back out soon. If I see Jimmy, I'll tell him to give you a call. How does that sound, Ms. Parrish?"

"That's good, Sherriff, and sir?"

"Yes, Ms. Parrish?"

"If you see him, you tell him I'm the lawnmower."

"Excuse me?"

"Yes, tell him his ass is grass, and I'm the lawnmower. He'll understand."

"I'm sure he will, Ms. Parrish. I surely will relay the message. Have a good night now."

Shaking his head, he hung up the phone.

# EIGHT

The sheriff turned to walk away, and the phone rang again. This time, he didn't have time to say a word before the caller began screaming. The woman on the other end of the line was talking so loud and so hysterically that he could not understand a word. When at last she took a breath, he responded.

"Miss, please start again, slowly and calmly. I can't understand what you're saying."

The woman tried again, but it was clear she was quite agitated.

"My husband, he's dead. He's dead!"

About then, Al entered from the back of the building. He was leading a handcuffed Tucker from behind, and the boy could barely manage to stay two steps ahead of him as he pulled up on the cuffs.

"Did I hear the phone?"

The sheriff held up a finger. "Tell me, ma'am, you say your husband has died. Can you tell me what happened?"

"I don't know. We were on the highway when he hit something with the car. It was like some kind of a puppet, the way it stumbled into the road... and the fucking thing exploded like a trash bag full of dog shit."

He could hear sniffling and crying for a moment before she continued.

"He told me to wait in the car, and he got out to see what it was. There was dark gooey stuff all over the car. He touched it... and that's when he started screaming. You should have seen his face. It swelled up so big, and then... and then *he* just exploded. There are pieces of him all over the front of our car. Did you hear me? He fucking exploded!"

He stood holding the phone. He had no idea what to say to that. Lana had just described the same phenomenon. Now here was another witness. Although she had not seen the trucker, she had experienced a separate but similar event.

"Where are you right now?" he asked.

"I'm inside of the car. I'm afraid to get out. I don't want to get that stuff on me. Wait a second, something is happening."

The phone went silent.

"Tell me what you see. Ma'am?"

His heart was pounding as he waited for her to get back on the line. When she screamed again, he nearly dropped the handset.

"The tires on the car just exploded, and there are a bunch of… of things… around the car. They look like plastic blow up girls, but, oh my Lord, they're walking! I think they're trying to get in the car. They keep bumping into it. They are throwing up that black liquid every time they hit. I'm trapped in here!"

"Lock the doors."

"They *are* locked. Please… please help me!"

"Can you tell me where you are?"

"No, uh, we pulled off the highway onto the side of the road. I don't have any…"

"Look out the window and tell me what you see."

"There is so much black goo I can hardly see out, and it smells horrible. Wait. I see a barn, Sheriff, a red barn with some kind of sign on the roof."

"I know where you are. You stay in the car, ma'am. We're on our way. Everything is going to be okay."

He was hanging up, as she was about to respond, "Everything is not going to be okay… my husband… Sheriff?"

The phone disconnected before she added, "Am I going to die?"

By now, the deputy and the boy were standing across the room, listening to him finish talking to the woman. Al opened his mouth to make a suggestion, closing it again when, without a word, Sheriff Wilson hurried to the gun cabinet on the wall and fumbled with his keys.

"Lana, Tucker, let's go."

"Where are we going, Daddy? Who was that?"

"Out by the Carpenter farm, there's a woman in a car saying her husband just exploded. What the hell is going on around here?" He shoved four shells in the chamber of the shotgun he was holding, and then racked one. "We need to get out there, she says she's trapped in her car."

He started for the door, but Tucker just stood there looking at Lana.

"Sheriff, I don't think we need to go..." He had a bad feeling about it. He didn't want to get involved in something that might get everyone killed, especially Lana.

"Look, punk. I don't know what's going on out there, but you two do. You think I'm going to let my only child stay here with you and get herself killed? No. So you better come along and maybe you can help me figure this thing out." He had one hand on the doorknob, and the other was holding the shotgun.

"But, sir..."

"Don't make me use this shotgun, boy. No matter what Lana said, you're still a robbery suspect. I could easily report that you were trying to escape." The look in his eyes spoke volumes.

"Daddy... what are you saying?"

"Okay... okay, just... come on." He didn't mean to say what he was thinking, but it slipped out. "I need your help."

"What about me?" Al was loading one of the other shotguns.

"Somebody has to stay here and man the phone. I'm afraid this isn't going to be the only call we get like this tonight. Keep me posted by radio." The sheriff let go of the door and turned his radio to full volume. "I won't be ignoring anything tonight. You let me know what the hell is going on if any more calls come in. I need you to do this, man."

Al couldn't hide his disappointment, but he couldn't argue. The sheriff had made a good case, and he was ready to fall in line as ordered. "Sure, boss. You be careful out there."

"You keep that shotgun by the desk in case you need it. Okay, Al?" He turned to the other two. "Let's go."

# NINE

To Lana, it seemed like forever before they reached the woman in her car. Actually, they had only been on the road a few minutes when they came upon the strange sight, and she whispered to Tucker, "Sorry I got us into this."

His attention was focused on the scene outside the patrol car. There were dozens of the things, people-like things, staggering to and fro on the highway, seemingly without any purpose or direction. It appeared that some were moving along the beams of the woman's headlights as though following a trail. Now that the sheriff had pulled up with flashing lights and sirens, the dolls started moving in their direction.

"Holy shit! Look at them. What in God's name is going on here?" He grabbed his microphone and flipped a switch. His voice broadcast from the speaker hidden under the hood of the patrol car. Very loudly, he asked the woman in the other car, "Are you all right?"

She turned her head around to look at them. Her mouth was moving, but they couldn't understand what she was saying, so he asked her, "Give us a nod if you are okay."

She nodded exaggeratedly, mouthing something they couldn't understand.

"I can't read your lips," he announced through the loud speaker.

The metal body of the woman's car was sitting close to the ground. There was no evidence that its custom rims had ever held rubber tires. The sheriff grabbed the handle of his spotlight, flipped it on and shone it on the vehicle. It looked as though it was covered with watered down tar.

"We're going to get you out of there, just hang on."

Out of nowhere, a few of the dolls bumped into the cruiser. Surprised, all three inside the vehicle screamed like little girls. The sheriff's face blushed with embarrassment. He had never shown fear in front of his daughter before. Then, there was the other problem. Not only were those things ugly as hell, some were anatomically correct and not something he wanted his daughter to see.

"What the fuck!" He was not going to sit around and be attacked. He shifted the cruiser into reverse and backed up twenty feet.

When the woman in the other car saw them backing up, she panicked. Frantically grabbing at the door handle to exit the car, she stopped as she realized that she was surrounded. Instead, she fumbled with the window handle and rolled it down a few inches, screaming through the gap in the window, "Don't leave me here!"

"Oh, Daddy, she thinks we're leaving her." Lana knew they had to stay, but in her heart, she wished they were leaving.

"We're not giving up, but we can't get out of the car with those things walking around like that. I need to figure this out."

Just then, in the beam of the spotlight, one of them spewed black liquid from its mouth about ten feet from the patrol car.

"What the fuck! That's where all that shit on her car came from?"

Again, the woman screamed, her hand grasping the top of the car window. "Please don't go. Help me!"

A glob of the dark fluid dripped from the top of the doorframe onto her arm. The pain was so intense that she forgot everything else, including the danger surrounding her. She threw open the car door and out she came, screaming and running toward the sheriff's car.

"Help... hhh..."

She began to swell. Pushing herself forward against the pain, she managed to get within five feet of the patrol car before she exploded. Blood and gore splashed onto the front end of the cruiser, and briefly, the light from the headlights cast a red glow on the horrific scene.

"Holy fuckin' shit!" Tucker yelled as he tried to reach from the back seat to throw the car in reverse. "Put it in reverse and get us the fuck out of here, Mr. Wilson!"

The sheriff did not hesitate. He took his foot off the brake, stepped on the gas pedal and pushed it all the way to the floor. The car shot backward into the darkness while a plume of blue smoke rolled up from the tires. With skilled hands, he turned the wheel and braked with his left foot as the cruiser did a one-eighty, sliding to a stop facing the opposite direction. Again, he floored it. Rubber melted to the pavement, and they shot down the road in the direction of town.

"What the hell am I supposed to do about something like that?" He spoke to no one in particular and stared straight ahead. "We're going to need help. I don't know who, maybe the FBI, or the Army, but I didn't learn anything about this shit in the academy."

"Sheriff, are you there?" screeched Al from the radio.

Lana grabbed the coiled cable and lifted the microphone from the floor where it dropped in the chaos.

"Go ahead, Al." She glanced over at the speedometer, catching her breath as she realized that they were reaching 90 mph.

"Miss Lana, tell your father that the phone is ringing off the hook here. People have been calling about animals exploding, alien dolls walking around on their property, and one guy said a... sorry... a dildo tried to jump him. A damn dildo!"

Lana stared at the radio wondering how she was supposed to respond to that. She didn't know what to say. The sheriff took the microphone from her hand.

"Anybody calls, you tell them to lock themselves in until they hear from us and... Al, I need you to call the VFD and tell 'em to sound the siren. There's a shit storm of trouble headed our way, and we're going to need all the help we can get to deal with it."

"What kind of shit storm are we talking about, boss?"

Al's voice betrayed his excitement. The most important thing he had ever been involved with was the time an escaped convict passed through town. The FBI had stopped by to ask some questions, but caught the suspect shortly thereafter. He had been disappointed that he did not have an opportunity to actually work on the case, but now, the strained tone in the sheriff's voice told him that this could be the big one.

"I... Fuck! I don't know, man. Just get the guys over there. I'm headed that way right now."

"You got it. You want me to stay here with the phone, or..." He crossed his fingers. "You want me to meet you at the fire station?"

"Get everybody you can find and meet us there. Oh, and tell anyone else you talk to not to engage at all with any of those strange dolls moving around town. Tell every family you see that they need to get to the nearest shelter as quickly as they can."

Slowing the car as he reached relative safety, he finished his thought. "Honest, Al, I don't know what the hell is happening out here."

Smiling, he answered, "Yes sir, I'm on it."

# TEN

Several minutes passed before the sheriff turned at the fire station. With tires screeching, they skidded into the parking lot. The small town had only two trucks and four men on duty. As the trio walked into the building, they were greeted by Bill Monroe, the fire chief.

"Well, hello, Sheriff. What brings you out tonight?" He added with a grin, "Where's the fire? Seems like you're in an awful hurry."

"Let's talk in your office, Bill. I've got something to tell you, and you're going to want to be seated when you find out what it is."

The chief led them into his tiny office. "Sorry, I don't have any extra chairs in here. We can get some from the storage room if you want." He took his seat behind his desk.

"No worries. This won't take long." The sheriff was shifting from foot to foot and glancing nervously through the window over the chief's shoulder.

"So what do you have for me, Hank?" His long time friend expressed true concern.

"Bill, you aren't going to believe this, but the kids here saw a tractor-trailer wreck earlier and... and... This is going to sound bat-shit crazy, but there was something on it..."

"Wild animals?"

"No." The sheriff took a deep breath. "Sex toys," he coughed the words out quickly.

"Uh... right. Like vibrators and...?

"I know it sounds crazy man," he interrupted, "but that's what we're dealing with out there tonight, a bunch of killer sex toys."

Bill was grinning. "Now that's a good one, but, uh, come on, what's really going on?"

There was a moment of silence until he realized that his friend had meant what he had said.

"You're not bullshitting me, are you, Hank? Vibrators?"

"No. Sorry to say this isn't a joke."

"So vibrators are headed toward town. Really? That's it? We could turn off the power.

You know, take the batteries out and shut the fuckers down."

"Well, I haven't actually seen any vibrators. So far, what we've run into are those inflatable love dolls, dozens of them. They attacked the cruiser and, Bill, I'm telling you, they killed a woman who was trapped in her car out on the highway right in front of us."

Bill slapped his hand to his forehead. "Holy shit! I mean, how the fuck does something like that even happen? Aren't those things made of rubber or something?"

"Vinyl – whatever. They're filled up with some kind of liquid, and they're walking around blowing that shit all over the place. It's some dangerous stuff."

There was some noise outside, and the sheriff went to the window to see where it was coming from. A man was walking across the parking lot away from his pickup truck and toward the side door of the station. Other than that, he didn't see any sign of trouble outside.

"It's Harry. I'll wait to fill in all the details. I don't want to have to tell this fuckin' story twice."

"I can understand that, considering the topic." Bill got up from his chair. "Love dolls, what the hell," he mumbled as he walked out of his office to greet his friend.

\*\*\*

A half hour or so later, the sheriff was standing at the back of a room filled with roughly twenty men. They had set up some chairs and were talking and laughing as they waited for him to begin. None had yet been told why they were gathered there. The sheriff had briefed Tucker and Lana how they should present the details of what they had witnessed. The pair had taken a seat with the others while they waited their turn to speak.

"Okay, guys, we need to get started," he announced as he moved to the front of the room. The chatter quickly subsided.

"I know you are all wondering why we asked you here at this late hour but, as I was telling Bill earlier, we have a major crisis on our hands. It's something that is going to sound so crazy I'm almost embarrassed to talk about it. That's why I'm going to start by letting my daughter's boyfriend, Tucker Peters, tell you how this all got started."

The teens looked at each other with stunned amazement. Her father had just called him her boyfriend. Lana had to nudge Tucker. Instead of moving to the front of the room, he rose from his chair and began to speak from where he stood.

"Hi, everybody, I'm Tucker."

"Louder," one of the men shouted. "We can't hear you."

He looked around to see who had spoken, then walked to the front of the room and cleared his throat. In a much stronger voice, he started again.

"I'm Tucker. Earlier tonight, Lana and me saw a... I mean heard a crash over by the highway. Um... I thought it was thunder but when we went to check it out, turned out, it was a big truck. It'd hit a tree."

The sheriff was getting frustrated with the pace of the boy's explanation. They needed to get out there and start hunting these things down. He didn't really have a good plan for dealing with the situation. He felt he it would be best to explain everything he knew about the threat before they went out to face it again. At least then, the men would know what they might encounter. After a few minutes more with the boy saying almost nothing, he interrupted.

"Thank you, Tucker. You can sit down."

Looking around the room at the faces of men he had known most of his life, he gathered his thoughts. These townsfolk were good strong people who took pride in their families, farms and small businesses. He knew they would do whatever was required, but he feared that some of them would not survive the night.

"Thanks for coming out tonight, guys. I know it's not easy to get called out like this in the middle of the night, and I appreciate you all being here. It's probably obvious that something serious is happening out there and, to tell you the truth…"

A man in the front row shouted, "Geezus, Wilson, cut the bullshit. Just tell us what the hell is going on."

The sheriff continued, jumping in with less than a well-planned statement. "Right, yeah, well, right now, out there, a damned tsunami of plastic tits and ass is headed our way."

He held up his hand as a low murmur and some laughter filled the room.

"Okay, now give me a minute here." He waited for the laughing to subside and continued, "Now, I'm not talking about a bunch of playboy bunnies or strippers, so don't get excited. It's love dolls we got out there, and they're killing folks. Might be thousands of 'em for all I know, and they're all over the place." He paused to be sure they understood he was serious.

There were a few grins, but no one said a word, except Jay Brock. "Love dolls? Damn, I guess my wife was right about them sex toy things being agents of the devil." He spoke with a serious tone and then burst out laughing. "Shit, Sheriff. You called us out here for that? Just turn the football team loose on 'em. We'll solve two problems with one solution, horny teenage boys and plastic hookers from hell. Them dolls will last about thirty minutes, I'm guessin'."

"Jay, how long have we known each other?" the sheriff asked, staring sternly at the man.

"Why, I'd guess goin' on forty years or so, Hank. Give or take a weekend or two."

"Right, and how often do you catch me pullin' pranks in the middle of the night?"

"Well, there was that one time at Mary Hart's house." Jay stopped to chuckle. "Remember when you put the dog shit in the bag and…"

"Holy mother and extended family, Jay! This here is some serious business. They are dangerous as hell and people are dying. If you'd seen what they did to that woman out on the highway, you'd keep quiet and let me finish." He raised his voice to emphasize, "Okay if I fucking finish, Jay?"

The man sat down in his chair. "Yeah, sure, Sheriff. You don't have to go off yellin' at a man. Go on."

"Here's what we know so far. The truck that the Peters boy was talking about was carrying some kind of liquid and it spilled out in the crash. It seems that the driver was exposed to whatever it was and then he exploded."

He paused to make sure everyone was paying attention, before going on. "Somehow, the dolls are filled with that liquid now, and it's probably what's brought 'em to life. Now that would be bad enough, but they are spewing it out all over the place. If I were a bettin' man, I'd say anything made out of rubber or plastic might be turned into a deadly weapon by that shit."

The atmosphere in the room had totally changed. Everyone was leaning forward in their chairs so as not to miss a word, so he continued, "We've been getting some calls about exploding animals, so I think we're dealing with the same shit there. If you get even a drop of it on you, you're likely to explode. That's one hell of a way to die, so I need some suggestions. I have no idea how to fight these things."

The silence in the room was deafening. Finally, one of the men spoke up.

"Shotguns. We can use buckshot, and blow them to pieces."

"That might work, but that will blow that liquid all over the place."

"How about fire? We could make a batch of Molotov cocktails and burn 'em to the ground."

"That could work, too, but we'll probably get some unwanted property damage. Keep in mind that gasoline fires are tough to put out once they get started."

The sheriff realized he wasn't going to get much in the way of new ideas. He'd already considered guns and fire. Any better ideas were not forthcoming.

"Maybe we should call the Army and ask for help." Tucker offered the suggestion, and it seemed to be the best idea yet.

"Maybe we should. More than likely, it was something of theirs on that truck," offered another man backing up the suggestion. "Sons-a-bitches always doing shit that gets civilians killed."

The group was in near unanimous agreement when Ben Wagner spoke up. "Fuck that! Haven't you seen any of those sci-fi monster movies? The Army drops a nuke on the town and claims it was a terrorist attack. No fuckin' way we call the Army to come out here. We need to deal with this shit ourselves."

The sheriff had to agree that what Ben said could be true. "So, that's it then. We have to do something to stop those things from getting into town. We're going to have to start with the shotguns and fire. If you came here without weapons, then you'd better head home and get whatever you've got. Meet me at the gas station in thirty, and bring any glass bottles you can find. Jars will work if you don't have bottles, but make sure they have lids for them. Bring rags, too. We're going to need to tear them up to make Molotov cocktails. If you have some fire extinguishers, bring those in case we set the fields on fire."

The men stood up and looked at each other in disbelief. If this was really happening, then they had to help. Otherwise, they risked losing everything.

"Let's go save the town!" he announced in his most positive sounding voice.

The group knew there could be no other choice. Although there was some grumbling, they headed for the door.

# ELEVEN

Pickup trucks and cars pulled away from the firehouse as the men headed for their homes. The plan to defend the town depended on an effective strategy. Unfortunately, they didn't have much to go on, and they were painfully aware of it.

Weapons, bottles, baseball bats and other supplies were gathered. Teenaged sons were awakened, and anyone who could pull a trigger or throw a bottle was rousted up. When they found all of the supplies they could, they made their way back to the town's only gas station.

Once there, they were met by the sheriff, Deputy Slater, Lana and Tucker. A map of the area was spread out on the hood of the sheriff's cruiser, and the officers and a couple of other men were looking it over in the light cast by several bright flashlights.

"I think we should split everyone into groups and assign them to a section of town." Al was always quick to give his opinion.

"You think?" The sheriff was looking off in the distance at the headlights coming toward their location. "We need to count the number of folks we have before we decide on anything. Some of those jokers don't seem to believe in the seriousness of our situation. Some might want to hang back and protect their own homes rather than come out to help everyone else, wait and see what happens. When they're all here we can decide what to do."

"Well, it figures," the fire chief spoke up. "I'm guessing Wagner will be one of them that don't come back. If anyone would wait around and cover his own ass, it'd be Ben Wagner. Remember the big grass fire? He sat on his porch with a garden hose waiting to see if the fire would get to his place."

"You don't need to remind me, Bill," the sheriff replied. "Let's give him the benefit of the doubt, though. I don't want to jump to judgment."

\*\*\*

The road seemed extra dusty as Ben headed for his house. In the distance, he could see his neighbors' lights and knew he was almost there. He lived some miles away from town and hoped to grab some guns and get back before everyone left without him. In his haste, he was driving faster than he normally would and forgot about the big dip in the dirt road.

Thrown about in his seat as he came upon it, his hands slipped from the wheel. The momentary loss of control sent his car sliding into the tall grass off the side of the road. As it came to rest, he threw it into reverse and tried to back out of the mess. He could hear the tires spinning behind him and opened the door far enough to lean out to see the problem. Sure enough, the quarter panel was covered with mud.

"Shit, not now."

Pulling himself up and back into the car, he put it in drive, and hit the gas. He planned to rock the car back and forth until he could get it to break free. To his dismay, it did not budge. Instead, he heard the tires spinning again.

"Fucking front-wheel drive!"

Ben pushed the door open again and climbed out.

"What am I gonna do now?"

He looked about in the shadows for something to shove under the tires for more traction, but found nothing. Swatting the tall grass around him, he grabbed a handful. Then he had an idea. Grabbing more and more grass, he pulled it from the ground by the roots. Once he had a large bunch of it, he shoved it under the front wheel on the driver's side.

He walked around the front of the car, pulling up more grass as he went. He planned to set a bundle under the other wheel. Midway between the headlights, he glanced up and found himself face to face with one ugly blowup doll. Its head was bald, and its face appeared to be haphazardly painted. The round blowhole of a mouth seemed to be mocking him as he blurted, "Oh, shit!"

Turning on his heel to run, Ben's foot slipped in the slick mud, and he tumbled face first to the ground. The doll blindly moved closer. He turned his head and watched its footless leg drag across the ground. Shuddering, it blew a stream of vile black liquid onto his back. He screamed in fear and rolled away from the thing.

Whatever had spewed from the vinyl abomination began to seep through his light cotton jacket. As he ran, he felt the fire on his skin. He was close to his house, so he broke into a full sprint, tearing off his jacket and throwing it to the ground.

In total panic, he bounded up the steps to his front porch, shrieking from the unbearable pain. It felt as though his head had swelled to twice its normal size and his vision was blurred. Reaching for the doorknob, his body exploded. What remained of him sprayed across the white aluminum siding of his tidy country home.

***

At the gas station, forty-some men and boys were busy filling plastic cans, glass bottles and jars with gasoline. Two men ripped long strips of old shirts and towels, shoving the rags into the waiting bottles and the holes that had been cut into the lids of the jars. The makeshift firebombs were then loaded into boxes to prepare for the assault that was yet to come. When all of them had been filled and boxed, the sheriff called out to the crowd.

"Alright, everybody, come on over here where you can see the map. It's time to get this love doll bitch-hunt started."

He waited while the large group gathered around before laying out his plan.

"I want everyone to get into in groups of four. Anybody who came here by car needs to ride out with someone who has a truck. I'll wait until you split up and get it sorted out."

He stepped back and waited, but no one made a move.

"Okay, let's try this. If you came here in a truck, raise your hand."

That got a response, and about a dozen hands went up.

"Alright, you guys with trucks step over there by the gas pumps. If anyone rode here with you, they should move over there, too."

He pointed toward the pumps in front of the building that doubled as a convenience store, and everyone who had raised their hands moved to the designated location.

"Now if any of these guys is a friend of yours, and you want to ride with him, go ahead and join him now."

With that, chaos ensued. About a quarter of the men moved to stand next to the fire chief. The sheriff shook his head. "Geezus, Bill. You seem to be the most popular guy at the dance tonight. I know you all hang out together, but some of the other guys could use some extra hands. Let's split this up a little more evenly, shall we?"

There was some grumbling, but the men moved to stand with the others until they were divided into groups of four.

"Much better. Now, I need the drivers over here. I'm going to give you your grid assignments."

He waved them over and turned back to the map.

"This is going to be tough. We've got a lot of ground to cover. Those things might be slow, but they've had a couple of hours to scatter since the wreck. Al, you take someone with you in your cruiser. Tucker and Lana will ride with me in mine."

"Are we going to split the map in half and command the groups in our sector? We can report progress with the radios."

Hank looked at his deputy with new respect. Rarely did anything of use come out of that reptilian brain of his, but here he was, making a lot of sense.

"That was a damn good idea."

The deputy's smile lit up the darkness. "Thanks, Sheriff, just doin' my job. I bagged and brought all of the extra radios from the station with me when I left for the firehouse, just in case."

"Al, old buddy, we're gonna have to talk about getting you a raise after this is over." He patted his deputy on the back and turned to continue his planning.

"Okay then. The highway pretty much splits our section of the county right down the middle. So, Al, you take everything on the east side from here to the cement plant." He took a pen from his pocket and drew lines on the map as he spoke. "We'll take the west side over to County Line Road."

By then, the other men had gathered around to try to get a look.

"Here's how we're going to roll." Sheriff Wilson stuck out his arm to split the men into two separate units. "From here to Paul over there on the end, your groups will be working with Deputy Slater on the east side of the highway. You'll be combing through the fields and woods as much as you can and obliterating any plastic piece of ass you see."

"My groups, from here to Craig over there, will be working the west side. We're going to start from here," he pointed to a road on the map, "and clear everything all the way down the highway back into town. Tucker, get that bag of radios out of the deputy's trunk for me." He tossed the boy his keys.

"Yes, sir."

Tucker ran to the rear of the cruiser and popped the trunk open as ordered. There was a black duffle bag lying next to a couple of shotguns and a Breathalyzer kit. He grabbed the handle of the bag and heard a rattling sound as he lifted it from the trunk. Jogging back to the group, he handed the bag to the sheriff.

The sheriff set it on the hood of the car and unzipped it. Fishing in the bag with his hand, he pulled out a handheld radio. He turned a knob on the top and tossed it to the man standing nearest to him.

"Here, we'll use these to stay in contact. Al, your group should tune to channel 6. We'll be on channel 8. You and I will relay on the main channel." He tossed one of the radios to the deputy and gave the bag to Lana.

"Hand these out, please, honey."

She took the bag from him and handed the radios out to the driver of each group.

"Oh, and there's one more thing. Bob, from the store here, donated these maps. He also wanted to let you know that the store will be open all night if you need snacks or drinks." He motioned toward the store. "Be sure to gas up before you leave. The gas is on the county, so fill those tanks to the top. Believe you me, nobody wants to get stranded out there tonight."

When the radios and the maps had been handed out, the group leaders gathered to mark their maps and get their assignments. Before long, they rolled out of the gas station to start clearing their designated areas.

# TWELVE

Al had been warned about the section of the highway where the previous attack had occurred. He had been cautioned against getting any liquid from the dolls on his tires, so he chose a surface road that ran horizontal to the highway in order to circumvent the area. The thought of the first victims' encounter with the animated dolls weighed heavily on his mind. The sheriff had said it had been a terrible mess.

"This is Deputy Slater. I'm nearly to the start point. Report your progress."

He spoke into the handheld radio tuned to Channel 6 and awaited a response as he rolled to a stop. A variety of clicks and sounds came from the radio, and then one man responded.

"This is Truck Two. We're in position on Flagstaff Road. My men are preparing to move out. Over."

Al was relieved to know they were finally getting things rolling. He hoped they would be able to wrap it up quickly so he could get home and check on his own family.

"10-4, Truck Two. Let me know if you see anything suspicious."

"We already seen 'em on the way here." The man sounded excited. "Wait a sec."

Al tried to respond, but the channel remained open. Evidently, the other man was holding his thumb on the transmitter button. The sound of gunfire caught him off guard, making him jump in his seat. He could hear the man yelling at someone, but couldn't make out what was said. When the man returned to the radio, his pitch had risen considerably. The fear in his voice was unmistakable.

"I gotta go, Deputy. Things are getting' kinda hairy here. Over and out."

Al felt his adrenalin surging. Nothing had gotten his heart pumping like this since old man Jacobs' bull got loose. After hours of chasing it, they had finally cornered it next to the fountain in the middle of the town square. It had been quite the ordeal and two men had been gored before the sheriff finally put it down.

Tonight was different. A lot of men were putting themselves in harm's way for their town and their families. It felt good to be a part of something big for a change, but if he were honest, he would have to admit that he was scared shitless.

"Trucks One, Three and Four, check in. I need your location." He held the radio near his mouth as he tried again. "One, Three and Four. I need your twenty."

Multiple voices shouted out from the speaker on his radio. He could hear rapid fire shooting. It sounded like all three trucks were trying to report in at once, but they were walking all over each other. There was a gunshot, and then another. He could hear echoes of shots in the distance. Suddenly, there was a flash of light a few miles away.

"Someone must be using one of the gas cocktails," he said aloud as he tried to calculate how far they were from the action.

\*\*\*

"Fuck! Rick, look behind you!"

The man was frantically pointing into the tall grass. The other man spun around to see what was coming.

"What? I can't see anything. The grass is too tall here."

There was a rustling sound, and he saw the grass moving. He leveled his shotgun and listened. A millisecond later, he fired a shot in that direction.

"Did I hit it?"

"I think so. There's nothing movin' over there now." He was standing in the bed of the pickup, loading three glass bottles filled with unleaded into a cloth sling bag. Carefully, he hung it over his shoulder.

"Gotta watch out for any movement in the grass, or they'll get up on you before you know it. The sheriff said they spray that stuff right out of their mouth, and you don't wanna get the shit on you, from what he said." He was talking to himself, but loud enough for the other man to hear, as he climbed down from the tailgate.

"Yeah, thanks." The man in the tall grass continued his sweep, using his shotgun to move the grass out of the way, as he walked along.

"Don't get too far out without signaling back, so's I know you're still there," the driver called to him from the cab of the pickup. "Just flash your light a couple of times to let me know where you are."

He shifted the truck into gear. "I'm gonna be rolling along with you at walkin' speed. See you on the other end." He was pointing toward County Line Road.

The other man grumbled as the truck headed out, "Maybe you could get your fat ass out here and help."

"I heard that. Yeah, bring your own truck next time, fucker. Then you can be team captain." He punched the gas and threw gravel from the tires into the night behind him.

\*\*\*

"Truck Three here. My men are out and moving. Took one of the bitches out so far. Over." There was a long pause before he released the button on the radio.

Al put the radio to his mouth. "10-4, Three. Be frosty."

"Huh?" The man in Truck Three was confused.

"Shit, man, be careful is all. Base out." He paused before he asked for Trucks One and Four again.

"Truck One here, almost to destination. The kid had to stop for a piss break." The voice was familiar, levelheaded and calm. "We've seen some movement, but nothing eyes on yet. It's as dark as an outhouse without a moon hole out here. Hoping the clouds clear soon. Over."

"Hang in there, One, the weatherman says it should clear up any minute. I'm going to clear the airwaves now. Base out."

"One out."

It was less than thirty seconds before all hell broke loose.

"This is Four." (*boom!*) (*boom!*) "We're surrounded! There are..." (*boom!*) (*boom!*) (*boom!*) "...hundreds out here." The sound clicked off, and then back on. "Throw the Molotov, don't hold it! Damn! What are those white things?"

Again, the sound was gone. That last statement rolled around in Al's brain as he waited for an update. Another long minute, and still there was nothing.

\*\*\*

The driver jumped out of the cab and into the back of the pickup, yelling, "Motherfucker!"

He had moved on the teenaged boy so quickly that he was shaking in fear. The angry man grabbed for the flaming gas bomb, and the boy panicked and dropped it. As the driver watched in slow motion horror, it fell straight into the box of other Molotov cocktails. The explosion threw the two of them over the side, into the grass, screaming, and on fire.

"Help me! I'm burning!" The boy shrieked as he rolled in the dirt at the side of the road. The older man was busy screaming and rolling around trying to put out his own fire. There was no time to be concerned with the boy.

Some fifty yards away, another crewmember had been clearing the field.

Before he saw flames shooting into the sky, he heard the yelling. It was obvious that it was coming from the road, and he began to push through the tall grass as fast as he could. He raised his shotgun over his head in order to move more quickly.

"I'm coming... hang on!" He yelled in the direction of the burning men.

# THIRTEEN

Al turned to the man who had chosen to ride with him. Carl King, the owner of the hardware store, was never one for a lot of conversation, but he was breathing hard now. The deputy was concerned that something was wrong with him.

"King, are you okay?" He checked the man's face for signs of a stroke. "What year is it?"

"You know what fucking year it is! Believe me, I'm okay. Just a pain in my shoulder is all. Nothing to worry about, Al." He rubbed his shoulder and did his best to force out a grin between tight lips.

"Look, you let me know if you need to get to a hospital. We're having enough problems tonight without you sitting here and dying on me." He grabbed the man's shoulder and gave it a reassuring squeeze.

"Shit, man! I just told you my shoulder hurts. What the fuck?" Carl leaned as far away from Al as he could.

"Oh, hell. Sorry, bud." Al's face flushed with embarrassment. "If you're alright, I'm gonna try to get hold of the guys again."

Before the man could answer, the radio crackled. "Truck One here. Over." The man sounded freaked out.

"There's more than those damn zombie dolls walking around out here. We got inflatable sheep too. I can't believe the crazy things people choose to fuck. If that ain't bad enough, I almost walked into a pack of dildos. Wait a minute, would that be a pack or a herd of dildos? I don't know, the fuckin' things are crawling along the ground like giant caterpillars. One of my guys tried to pick up a double headed two-footer. He was screaming loud enough to break glass before he exploded like a popped balloon!"

The man breathed heavily into the radio. It sounded like he was running. "We used gas bombs on the walkers and they burned real good, but there's too many to get 'em all like that. We're just about out of gas, and shooting at 'em hardly slows 'em down. If you don't hit them in the right place, the shot just pushes 'em around. What do you think we should do? Over."

Al was speechless. He had expected the whole roundup to last an hour or so. Things were spinning out of control, and it was beginning to sound like a lot of men were paying with their lives.

"This is Mike! Can anybody hear me?" Another voice screamed through the radio. "I'm with Truck Four, and my team is down. Nobody is left but me, and now the fuckin' truck is on fire. I can't get..." The radio clicked, and there was silence.

"Oh, shit! Come in, Four..." Al felt his heart pounding. "Four, where are you?"

"Headed for the highway..."

From the sounds he made, Al could tell that he too was running. He was holding the transmit button down, so the deputy couldn't answer.

"Can someone come and... shit, they're everywhere. Oh, god, I've been hit! It sprayed... I'm..." He fell to the ground as he finished his sentence, "...on fire!"

There was a sound of a wet explosion, and then silence.

# FOURTEEN

"Sheriff, this is Al, do you copy?"

The radio broke the silence in the cruiser. Lana had been just about to drift off to sleep in the back seat. The yelling startled her, causing her to jump.

"Go ahead, Al. What do you have…"

"Hank, I'm losing men here fast. Those fuckin' things are everywhere on this side of the highway. I think I've lost two trucks already. Can you see flames from where you are?"

The sheriff adjusted his rear view mirror until he saw the glow from the fires. "Yes, I have a visual."

Clearing his throat, he instructed his deputy. "Listen. Get your men out of there, head back to town. We'll meet you at the bar. Do you copy?"

"On it. I'll get back to you." The radio fell silent.

"This is out of control. Does anybody see anything?" The sheriff twisted in his seat to look all around them.

"I don't see anything, Dad. It's too dark."

"Tucker?"

"No, sir. Nothin' yet."

He grabbed the handheld radio off the console. "Trucks One through Four, report in on my count. Go, One."

"This is Truck One, over."

"What are you seeing out there, One?"

"We've seen a few dolls. We took 'em out with the shotguns. Pretty quiet here now. Over."

"Head back to town, One. There's been a lot of damage to the other trucks, and we need to regroup. Meet us at the bar. Copy?"

"Copy that, Sheriff. Getting my men now. One out."

"Two, do you copy?" There was nothing but silence in return. "Truck Two, do you copy?"

The ominous silence was more than worrisome. There was no way to tell if anyone in Truck Two was still alive.

"I'm turning this thing around."

The sheriff threw the car in gear and began a wide turn across the lanes of the highway.

"Holy shit!" Tucker pointed through the windshield at several dozen dolls that had nearly reached the spot where they had just been parked.

The sheriff put the pedal to the floor.

"Hang on!"

The cruiser fishtailed through the rest of the turn. The car turned so quickly, he didn't see the walkers that had already reached the pavement. As he plowed through them, they exploded. The black liquid that had brought them to life splashed over the car like a five-dollar car wash.

"Fuck!"

The foul smell infiltrated the air vents of the car. He continued down the road for another sixty yards. It was as far as they could go before the tires began to screech. Smoke billowed out from the wheel wells as the tires took on a life of their own and the trans-axels of the car snapped with a loud, *"Krrack!"* Seconds later, the cruiser jerked to a stop and reversed direction on it's own.

"Dad, what's happening?" Lana yelled. "We're going backwards..."

Simultaneously, all four tires exploded with a loud "Bang!" The body of the car dropped level with the pavement and the car came to a complete stop.

"We've got to get out of here!"

Tucker grabbed for the door handle, as Hank reached for the handheld radio, picking it up from the floor where it had fallen when he made the turn.

"Wait! Don't open that door. We've got to get some help. We can't just walk out of here." He pressed the button on the radio. "Any truck, repeat, any truck out there, we are stranded. Need help, right now!"

There was no response.

"Dad, we can't die like this!" Lana yelled. "This is so fucked up!"

Tucker turned to reach for her, but jammed his hand into the grate that separated the front seat from the back.

"Shit, I forgot about that damn thing. I'll get you out of here, baby."

He pressed his fingers through the grid, and she reached for him.

"Seriously? *Baby?* I should kick your ass for getting us into this mess," the sheriff yelled at him.

The radio crackled to life. "Turn on your emergency lights, Sheriff. We're headed your way."

Hank reached over and flipped on the red and blues. "They're on."

Through the back window of the car, Lana could see a line of walking death advancing in their direction.

"Hurry! They're almost on us!" The sheriff was yelling into the microphone.

"I'm a minute away!" the voice on the radio screeched.

"I see them. Thank you, Jesus!" Lana expressed her relief as she watched the bright fog lights of the pickup truck closing in on them.

When the truck stopped a few yards in front of the disabled car, two men jumped from the back with red canisters in their hands. They began spraying the ground around the car with fire extinguishers.

"Don't get out until we spray the car," the man on the radio ordered. "When I say go, get out and run like hell. Jump in the bed of our truck."

The men with the fire extinguishers held the nozzles up and covered both sides of the car with clouds of white icy fog. When Tucker touched the window, he could feel the cold. "They're using $CO_2$!"

"Go!" the voice from the radio yelled.

In unison, all three doors opened. The sheriff and teens jumped out and ran for the truck, as the men with the fire extinguishers followed close behind them. The tailgate was dropped to make it easier for them to climb in, and Tucker reached for Lana, lifting her up before pulling himself up with help from one of the men. Once Hank had scrambled up onto the truck bed, one of the other men got into the cab with the driver. The other stayed with the three in the back, closing the tailgate as the truck began to move.

"Everyone stay seated. It could be a rough ride," the man told the three of them. "We saw some of those dolls on the way here, and we may have to run off the road again."

"What was with the fire extinguishers?" Tucker asked him.

"We grabbed them when we were at the fire station and brought them along because of the gas bombs. Found out that liquid stuff gets thick, almost solid when it gets cold. We used it to stop that black shit from dripping on you while you got out of the car. Cool, huh?"

"That's pretty smart. Do you think we could fight those things with cold?" Maybe it was the answer the sheriff had been seeking.

Just then, the driver stuck his head out the window. "Where are we headed?"

"Back to town. Head to The Pike. We need to regroup and evaluate our losses."

The sheriff sat down in the truck bed just in time. The driver hit the gas and high-tailed it toward town.

# FIFTEEN

On any typical night, Kensington would shut down by 11 p.m., dark and quiet. The exception to the rule was The Pike, a small biker bar situated on the edge of town. It was the only place open until 2 a.m., except on Saturday nights when they closed at midnight in an attempt to encourage attendance at church the next morning.

The traditional neon beer signs cast a surreal red and blue glow on the ground outside the bar's only window. As the pickup skidded into an empty spot in the gravel parking lot, six people piled out of it and rushed into the bar. A handful of patrons intent on staying until closing time were shooting pool and playing video games while *Don't Fear the Reaper* blasted from the speakers of the CD jukebox in the corner.

The crew that had rescued the sheriff's party went straight for the bar and, before anyone could say a word, three shots of Jack Daniels were lined up in front of them. Waiting, nervous hands were ready to throw them back and ask for another. The sheriff stopped just inside the door and looked around. He headed toward the source of the music, pulled it away from the wall and yanked the plug.

"Hey, what the fuck?" one of the guys playing pool shouted as the song halted just before the chorus. "That's my fuckin' dollar, bitch! You shouldn't a oughta done that. Mo... ther... fucker!"

He walked toward the sheriff, who was bent over and pushing the jukebox back to the wall. The rough looking character shifted the cue stick in his hands to hold it like a baseball bat. Sensing the movement behind him, the sheriff spun around to face the man.

"Just step back and give me a minute, Garrett. There's some shit going down tonight and we need your help." He looked around the bar at the dozen or so biker types. "I see the ladies have gone home already. That's good 'cause we are gonna need all of you to pitch in."

"Is that you, Sheriff Wilson?" the bartender asked from across the room. "I figured it would take someone with a lot of balls or just some crazy bastard to walk in here and unplug my jukebox."

He pulled his hand from beneath the bar and laid the aluminum baseball bat down on top of it. "So what do you need our help with tonight?"

One guy, who had been in the rescue truck, began, "You aren't going to believe this shit, but I'm tellin' you, we've seen it for ourselves. We lost Max out in the field tonight."

The sheriff was walking through the room looking at the next round of recruits, wondering if they would be willing to volunteer or if they would have to be pressured.

"He's right about that. We've lost good men out there trying to keep the terror from reaching town, but we couldn't stop them."

Everyone there, but the bartender, was at least three sheets to the wind. He had his doubts about the value this buzzed up crew might have, but he knew he had no choice. He had to enlist their help.

"The fuck you guys talkin' about?" The man who had made the challenge before he realized he was talking to the sheriff, now lowered his pool cue.

"This is going to sound crazy, like the man said," the sheriff said, as he pulled out a barstool and sat down. "Earlier tonight, a semi-truck full of strange cargo had an accident out by the highway. What came out of that trailer has killed several men, probably some of your friends, and some local livestock. I hate to tell you this, but they're headed this way."

He paused, trying to think of a way to say it was sex toys without sounding like a lunatic, but Al had come into the bar while he was talking and said it for him.

"It's hundreds – maybe thousands – of sex toys, blow-up dolls, and dildos."

The deputy had blurted it out, but his lack of emotion failed to illustrate the seriousness of the situation. One of the bearded men burst out in laughter, blowing a mouthful of beer across the pool table and into the face of the guy standing on the other side. Before a fistfight could break out, the sheriff backed up the statement.

"That's what I was talking about. What my deputy just told you is true. It's turned into a damn invasion of killer sex toys." The sheriff crossed his arms. "Any questions before we figure out what we do next?"

"I got one," the bartender volunteered. "These things are killing folks, right?" He looked around at his motley group of customers and said with a grin, "What are they doin'? Fuckin' 'em to death?"

The laughter died away when the men saw that the sheriff wasn't smiling.

"I should've known better than to come here. It's hard enough to talk sense to a drunk about anything normal like driving under the influence, but telling you that some of your friends have been killed by sex toys? I understand it's a real stretch. Unfortunately, we're not bullshitting you."

It was clear now that this was not a joke, and the questions began to fly.

"So what do you expect us to do? You already went out there and got your asses kicked, and you have more authority than we do, and more firepower, I'm guessin'."

"Yeah, I'm on probation. I ain't allowed to even look at a gun."

One of the heavily tattooed guys volunteered, "If it's an invasion of some sort, why not call the Army and let them handle it? Isn't that their job?"

A bearded man stepped forward. "No, you don't call in the feds. They'll nuke the whole area trying to cover this up. Haven't you seen what they do in those movies? We have to handle this shit ourselves. What do you want us to do, Sheriff?"

"Ole Ben Wagner made the same comments about the Army…"

The sheriff was cut short when Carl ran through the door, yelling, "Fuckers are headed this way!"

# SIXTEEN

By the time everyone had assembled in the parking lot, the roaming dolls were less than fifty yards away. They blindly stumbled down the street, intermittently spewing putrid black fluid from every orifice of their synthetic bodies. The sight of them took the drunken newcomers to the situation by surprise.

"Holy hell! Look at that. How are them things even walking around and shit?" The guy who had spoken up took off his baseball cap and scratched his head. "It's like a nightmare, but I don't think I'm sleeping."

Grabbing hold of his beard, he pulled to see if he could feel any pain. He was certain that he would not feel anything if it were a dream. "Fuck, that hurts! I can't believe this shit is real."

"We aren't sure what's causing them to move like that, but you see it now with you own eyes. Be careful not to get any of that liquid shit on you, or it'll kill you real quick like. I'm pretty sure it's what brought them to life." Sheriff Wilson knew he had their attention now, and they were running out of time. He got straight to business. "If any of you have weapons in your cars or trucks, now would be the time to get them."

He looked over at Al. "Get those trucks out there and line 'em up. We might not be able to stop them all with shotgun pellets, but maybe we can slow them down. It could buy us some time to try something else."

The deputy jumped into action, singling out several men. "You, you, and you... you too, get your trucks and line them up across the street."

When the men were in their trucks, he stepped out into the narrow street and motioned with his arms how he wanted them to form the line. "Don't leave more than a foot of space between the bumpers, or they'll squeeze through."

The men revved their engines and pulled into the street. After a bit of maneuvering, they had successfully blocked it from building to building.

"Everybody with guns, get over there by the trucks. Take out as many of those things as possible before they reach the barrier. Shoot low and blow out their legs. That should keep them from coming any closer. I don't think they can stay inflated with that much damage to the body."

The sheriff knew that this motley group would not be enough to stop all that would be coming their way. He just wanted to buy some time until he could come up with another way to resolve the situation.

One of the men headed to the barrier carrying a machete. "Shouldn't we cut off the heads? That's how they kill 'em in the TV shows."

Tucker was coming up behind him carrying a shotgun. He answered, "If you cut its head off with that blade, you'll get black shit all over you. One drop of that stuff and you're done for. You'll explode."

"Okay then, gimme that shotgun of yours and go get yourself another one. Seeing as how you're all friendly with the law out here tonight, it should be easy for you."

Tucker hesitated. While he gave the suggestion some thought, the others had taken up their positions and begun firing away. The men were whooping and hollering with each successful hit. Meantime, the machete guy was starting to look pissed.

"Come on, kid. I'm missing out on the action. Give it up and that box of shells too." He pointed at the box tucked under the boy's arm. Reluctantly, Tucker handed over the gun and ammo. The man snatched it from his hands and ran to join his friends.

Sheriff Wilson and Deputy Slater watched from the sidewalk as, one by one, the dolls were cut off at the legs by shotgun pellets. It seemed as though the strategy might work, and Al was beginning to feel better about their chances of survival. At the end of the line of shooters, two men were standing in the bed of their truck. They seemed to be lighting something that looked like fireworks, and sparks were flying from the burning fuse.

"What the hell?" Al yelled for them to stop.

As though in slow motion, he watched as one man's arm cocked back and let it fly. It was then that he recognized the stick of dynamite. At the same time, he was diving for cover, yelling, "Everybody get down!"

The dynamite was tumbling end over end into the center of about a dozen advancing dolls. Sparks jumped from the burning fuse as the dynamite bounced on the ground. Before anyone could turn to see the threat or take cover, a huge explosion shook everything down the block. It blew the windows out of buildings and set off alarms everywhere.

The sheriff could see the blast from where he stood. It threw a raining death of black droplets toward the line of trucks and the men. Exposed to open air, the fluid expanded. By the time it reached the blockade, it rained heavily on the men, as well as the trucks they were using for cover. No one who had taken a position near the trucks was spared. Even the men who had tossed the dynamite became victims of their own stupidity.

Within seconds, the screaming began. Some tried to run while others writhed on the ground. Moments later, exploding bodies cast a red hue beneath the streetlights. The disgusting chorus of bloated, wet popping sounds replaced the screams of the dying. In less than a minute, bits of flesh and chunks of meaty skeletons were all that remained of many of the men who had volunteered to help them.

All those who had not been exposed to the toxin watched in shock as it unfolded before their eyes. Groaning at the loss of his friends, one man found his voice and began yelling, "Fuck this, fuck this," as he ran for the town square.

As though the red death of exploding men wasn't bad enough, strange sounds began to emanate from the trucks, which suddenly began to move erratically. They bumped into each other and began moving out of place.

"Shit, it got on the tires," the sheriff moaned as the line of closely parked trucks slowly shifted and turned, leaving large gaps between them. "Everybody load up and get out of here. We're headed to the square."

He was already walking toward the open door of the cruiser. "Do whatever you feel you have to, but if you want to help us stop these things, meet us there."

He grabbed Lana's hand and dragged her toward the deputy's car. "Come on, Al, we need to take your cruiser. You too, Tuck. Move it, now!"

Behind them, the tires began to burst. The loud popping sounds echoed in their ears as their car doors were slammed shut and they headed toward the center of town.

# SEVENTEEN

In the town square, most of the men who had survived the incident outside the bar assembled near the old World War II statue. The sheriff stood near the commemorative plaque silently reading the words on the plaque before turning to face the crowd.

"Men, tonight we must decide whether to stand and fight for our town or to walk away and get help from the outside." He motioned toward the statue. "Our fathers and grandfathers fought bravely during the big wars for their home and country. It was an enemy they understood, man and machine against an evil regime. They didn't back down in the face of danger, but charged ahead, regardless of the risk. All those who survived returned home as heroes."

"Those men had primitive weapons by today's standards and an army of thousands behind them." Al had been listening intently, but he doubted that there was even a chance of winning this fight. "All we have are some shotguns and bottles of gasoline, and that's not proving to be all that effective. We're sure as hell not going to try to fight these things with our fists."

He stepped toward the men and finished his thoughts. "I think it's time we abandon the town and call the National Guard in to clean up this mess. We can come back when it's over and rebuild. Hopefully, there will be something left to come home to."

The faces of the men reflected the doubt they were feeling. They, too, had no expectations of being able to pull off a victory against such an enemy. Most had families at home and they were increasingly concerned for their safety every moment this futile battle continued. Many were considering retreat, though they had not yet voiced their feelings. They hoped to get their families and head out of town, if it wasn't already too late.

"I vote we can get to our families and get the fuck out of Dodge. Let the military handle it. It's their job to deal with this kind of shit, not ours." The man in the baseball cap looked around at the others. "We don't even know for sure what we are fighting out here. Yeah, we know they're sex dolls, but how are they walking around terrorizing the place? We don't know, and you don't have any real answers. This whole thing is bullshit."

"Arthur's right," another man decided to weigh in. "We saw them guys explode back there. What the hell have you gotten us into here? Maybe if we'd stayed at the bar, if you hadn't come there and got us all riled up, those other guys might be alive right now. I say, fuck it, let's get out of here."

The sheriff didn't blame the men for doubting their chances of success in this fight. He had lost all but a sliver of confidence the moment the dynamite had exploded. He decided to take a vote to find out if everyone was on the same page.

"I need a show of hands..."

Before he could say anything else, every hand shot towards the night sky.

"I was going to ask for a show of hands of any who think we should stay and fight."

The hands slowly retreated.

His heart sank. The men had decided to give up before he even appealed to them for one last assault on the invaders. He couldn't blame them, but there was no way he could face this threat alone. Maybe it *was* time to run. All he had to do was say the word, and everyone would abandon the town. He hated to give up without giving it one more try.

"Alright, I know how you feel. I lost some lifelong friends out there, just as you all did. If we leave now, everything we have worked our entire lives to achieve may be lost, but worse than that, the sacrifice our friends and neighbors have made here tonight will have been in vain. You all need to be sure about this. If we decide to leave without stopping these things, we may never be able to return."

"Come on, let's get the fuck out of here." It was the guy in the cap again. Without further hesitation, he and his friend turned and ran toward their truck.

"So I need to know, are we going to stay, or should we go?" The sheriff took his hat off, smoothed his sweaty hair and placed it back on his head. He didn't have to wait long for their answer.

Almost as one, the men shouted the word, "Go!" They nearly tripped over each other in a mad dash to their vehicles. Keys turned, engines chugged, and they made for the side streets in all directions leading out of the square.

Sheriff Wilson, Lana, and Tucker stood alone in the glow from the park's lights. Al had abandoned them and headed for home with one of his neighbors.

"What now, Daddy?" Lana was holding Tucker's hand close to her chest as though somehow he could protect her.

"We don't have a choice, honey. We've got to go now."

# EIGHTEEN

Al's patrol car was parked across the street on the other side of the small park. As the sheriff and the two teens moved toward it, tires screeched and headlights approached from one of the side streets. The pickup was traveling at such a high rate of speed that, when it turned the corner, it looked as though it would flip over. One of the tires exploded, and the driver lost control. The truck slammed into the patrol car, crushing the driver's side door. Instantly, the car was rendered un-drivable.

The trio ran to offer assistance, but by the time they reached the crash, the driver and passenger were stumbling away from the wreckage. To their dismay, they recognized Al and his neighbor.

"They're fucking everywhere!" Al was holding his left arm as it hung limp at his side.

"Are you hurt? What did you see?" Tucker asked, as he led the other man to one of the wooden benches that lined the park and helped him to sit down.

"What? No, I'm okay. My knee hit something pretty hard."

The man appeared to look right through the boy. "Those things... the dolls... They were coming into town from that direction. When we cut down a side street to go around them, they were there, too. When we backed up to get away from them, we ran over a bunch of crawling rubber dicks... I mean dildos. They were moving across the ground like fucking inchworms."

Al interrupted to add to the story. "I'm guessing the tire that blew out got some of that black shit on it. He was having trouble steering, and then it exploded. He tried to stop, but he lost it."

"We're all stranded now," Lana cried out. "How are we going to get away with the car smashed up like that?"

"Wait, I think I hear another car coming." Tucker headed toward the sound of the approaching vehicle. He ran across the street at the end of the square and looked to his left. Panic gripped him when he saw a half dozen dolls stumbling along in his direction. There was a splashing sound as one of them spewed its deadly venom on the pavement. The truck pulling up at the corner got his attention when the driver rolled down his window and yelled at him.

"That way is blocked. There's a car flipped over and those things are stumbling around it puking black shit all over the rest of the street. There's no way out of here!"

His eyes were wide with panic as he stepped out of the truck and walked toward the others who were standing around the park bench. Tucker followed him, and before long, there were more headlights as other vehicles drove into the square.

"Looks like everyone is coming back." The boy sounded defeated. Within minutes, most of the men who had tried to leave town had returned. They gathered around the sheriff.

"What do we do now? We can't leave!" one of them yelled, his voice straining with fear and anger. "Those things will be swarming here any minute."

"We need to get off the street before that happens." The sheriff looked around for a building that might be a good refuge from the coming wave of death spewing blowup dolls. "We're going to have to break into one of these stores."

"We don't have to break into anything. I have the keys to the drugstore." A man held some keys over his head. "We can hide in there until dawn. Once we have a clear view of what's out here, we can figure out what to do next."

The sheriff recognized James Fisher as the man with the keys. He had worked at the drugstore part-time since he lost his job at the car dealership. The bad economy and decreased sales had finally put the place out of business. Working at the store had been his last hope.

"Sounds like a plan, James. Lead the way."

Sheriff Wilson beckoned everyone to follow, then reached for Lana's hand. She and Tucker hurried along with him across the square to the small store. James inserted his key in the lock and opened the door. There was an alarm keypad just inside the door. He punched in the code, before reaching to switch on the lights.

"Maybe we'd better leave the lights off for now. We don't know if the light attracts those things."

"You may be right. I have some chairs in the back if anybody needs one, or you can just pull up a piece of floor." James went to the back room to fetch some chairs.

"So what's the plan now, Sheriff?" one of the men asked. "Are we going to sit here until those things move on? By then, that black shit will be all over the place, and we won't be able to drive or walk anywhere."

Almost as though to prove his point one of the love dolls came scraping along the front window of the store. It let loose a blast of noxious black fluid on the sidewalk directly in front of the door.

"Dad, look at this!" Lana was watching out the window as the doll walked by.

"What is it?" He joined her at the front of the store and saw what she was pointing out. "Oh, God. We never stuck around long enough to see that happen."

"What is it?" The rest of the men pushed forward to see what was going on outside the window.

Before their eyes, the puddle of black liquid on the sidewalk was growing larger. It bubbled, seeming to rise up from the sidewalk. The group watched in fear and awe as it spilled over the curb and into the street. When several ridges suddenly extended upward into finger-like points, they jumped away from the window.

"Holy shit! It's alive," gasped Al as he walked backwards into one of the aisles. "And growing!"

"That must be what causes people to explode. After it absorbs into the skin, it expands just like that. A person can only expand so far, then they burst." The sheriff sensed the men's growing desperation after what they had seen. "I thought we could wait this out, but by this time tomorrow, there could be a river of that shit flowing down Main Street."

"Well, what do we do now?" Tucker was holding a push broom in front of him as though he thought it might help keep the killer dolls at bay.

"What about cold?" Lana remembered that the cold from the $CO^2$ fire extinguishers that had prevented the toxin from dripping on them when they were trapped in the patrol car. "Remember when we were trapped..."

"Yes, but we don't have enough of those extinguishers in this whole town to fight all of these things. They have been spreading that shit everywhere, and if all of it spreads like what we just witnessed out there, we won't be able to walk outside at all without stepping in it." The sheriff turned to James, "Do you have any of those extinguishers here in the store?"

"We have at least one in the back, I think. I'll go get it." He headed for the storeroom in the back of the store.

"It won't save the town, but it might save *us* if things get any worse." Sheriff Wilson turned to address the rest of the group. "We should stay away from the windows. I don't know what attracts them, but we shouldn't take any chances." He held his arms out and began moving everyone toward the back of the store.

# NINETEEN

There was an hour left before dawn, and the remaining survivors huddled in the drug store, discussing what to do when morning came.

"Hank, I want to call home and make sure my wife's still okay. It bothers me to say that things got hairy so quickly, I never checked on her. I guess I was thinking I would get home to her before this."

Al was on the verge of tears, not simply out of worry for his wife and child. He was beginning to think that none of them would make it through the night.

"Sure, buddy. I'm guessing there are others here who want to call home. Here, use my phone." He handed his phone to the deputy. "Anybody else here need a phone to call home?"

Half a dozen hands went up. He was surprised that so many of them were without mobile phones, but after all, it *was* a small town. Most of the younger adults and teens carried them, but older folks kept their old technology. It was what they knew and, for many of the men trapped in that store, it was good enough.

The sheriff called to the back of the store where James was staying busy with a broom and a dustpan. "Hey, James, do you have a phone back there that these guys can use to call their families?"

"Sure thing, Sheriff. Anybody who needs to use the phone, step right this way."

He led the men to the small office in the back of the store. Meanwhile, Al was dialing his home number for the third time. He let out a sigh of relief when someone finally answered. The sheriff could hear his side of the conversation.

"Julie, honey, where's mommy? Tell her I need to talk to her."

"What?"

"She what? No, No. Stay in the house, honey. Don't go outside." He held the phone to his chest and tears streamed down his face. Putting the phone back to his ear, he assured his daughter, "Daddy is coming. Stay in the house, honey. Is Barney still in the house? Don't let him out, and don't open the door no matter what. Daddy is on his way. I'm coming." He pressed the button to end the call and handed the phone back to the sheriff.

"Al, you can't…"

"Fuck you, Hank! You have your daughter here with you. Mine saw her mother killed by those fucking things!"

Before Hank could stop him, the deputy dropped the phone and was out the door. He jumped over the pool of black fluid that had spread over most of the sidewalk and ran for an abandoned truck that was parked on the other side of the square. A door was hanging open and the ding, ding, ding sound coming from it made it clear… the keys were in the ignition.

"I can't believe I didn't see that coming. I could have stopped him." Hank was pacing as Al got in and took off in the direction of his home. He felt sick knowing that the poor guy might never make it to his house, but he didn't blame him for trying.

Unfortunately, the deputy's act of loyalty to his family started a chain reaction. When the sheriff bent down to pick up his phone, three other men bolted out the door and ran for their trucks. One of them wasn't as lucky as Al. When he tried to jump across the pool of black ooze outside the door, he landed right in the middle of it.

Hank wasn't sure if he was seeing things, but it looked to him like black tendrils shot up the guy's leg when he landed. A few seconds later, after screaming and gesturing wildly at them through the window, he exploded. The men in the store groaned and stepped back as red bits sprayed the plate glass window.

"Now what, Sheriff? We just gonna sit here? We need to get help. Call the Army, for fuck's sake!"

The man stared at him, waiting for a response, but Hank was still gawking at the bloody particles of what was once a man, sliding down the glass.

"Fuck this, I'm calling them."

The man ran for the phone in the office. When Hank finally snapped out of it, Tucker was pulling at his shoulder.

"Mr. Wilson, Sheriff, Hank! He's calling the Army. Remember what you said would happen?"

"I know, son, but we are out of options. I'd better talk to the feds. They're going to want some official verification before they send help."

Reluctantly, he walked toward the office where the other man was still waiting for the 411 operator to provide the number.

"Hang up. I have the number in my cell. I'll call them directly."

The man pushed the button on the phone to end the call and handed the phone to the sheriff. "I'm sorry, I…"

Hank held his hand up and pulled his phone from his pocket. "Don't apologize. I probably should have called them when this all first started. I just thought that I… I mean that we could fucking handle it. I was so wrong."

He held out the phone and scrolled through several numbers in the directory before he found the number for Fort Martin. He clicked to dial it and waited.

"Fort Martin, Lieutenant Mackey speaking."

"Mack, it's Hank. I… I don't know how to say this, but some terrible shit has hit the fan here in Kensington."

"Hank, what's the problem? You sound pretty upset."

"Look, you won't want to believe this, but my town is under siege. We're being attacked by walking and crawling killer sex toys."

The soldier choked on the coffee he had just sipped when he heard what his friend had said. "Hank, what the fuck are you folks smoking over there? Why are you making crank calls at the ass crack of dawn?"

"Look, man, this is not a crank call. A truck wrecked here last night, and I don't know what the guy was hauling, but I assume it was some of your military bullshit. Whatever it was, it made the whole shitload of sex dolls, and every other sex toy that guy was hauling come to life. They're walking around spraying black liquid all over the place. People are exploding.

If the shit touches you even a little, you're fucked. I don't know for sure how many people have been killed already. I need your help, Mack. Right fucking now." The sheriff was pleading with his friend.

"Okay, calm down, man. I need to make a couple of calls. I'm going to put you on hold. Okay?"

"Sure... but, hurry. We're trapped in the drugstore over here, and the dolls are swarming. They're everywhere."

# TWENTY

The sheriff never would have guessed that the Army would have music on hold, some of the worst elevator music he had ever heard. A variation of *Love is a Battlefield* played on a loop, a surreal soundtrack for the long night of deadly assault he and the others had been trying to survive.

After what seemed like forever, the man came back on the line.

"Hank, you still there?"

"Yeah. Are you sending some troops out?"

"Uh... yeah. Look, man, I have to go."

"What? What's going on?"

"Can't say, Hank. This line isn't secure, but... remember when we were kids jacking copper wire along the railroad tracks? You cut that wire, and it hung down over Niles Road. That pickup came past with the rack of fog lights. You remember how it caught the wire in the lights, damn near tearing them off, and what you said to me when you jumped down from the pole?"

The sheriff made a face and thought for a second before replying, "Uh, I think I said, we need to get the fuck out of here. I think I started yelling, "Run…"

"Yeah, that sounds about right. Good luck, man." The phone went dead.

Hank was stunned. Had he just been warned to run by his old friend, someone he trusted? Was it true, what he had been hearing all night about the military? Were they actually going to nuke the town? If that was so, there was no time and no way to know for sure. He had to do something, or they were all going to die here in the drugstore.

"Listen, everyone." He was walking down one the aisles of the store. "Does anyone have a truck that's still in working order?"

Three men stepped up. "I do," they said.

"We don't have time to discuss it, but I think this town is going to be wiped out, nuked or otherwise. We need to try to get to those trucks and get out of town, and we better go right now."

Just as he got the words out, another doll came bumping along the front of the building, spewing its foul payload all over the plate glass window of the store. The streetlights outside grew dim as the black fluid ran down to the base of the window and stopped at the silicone seal that held it in place.

Lana had been on watch as her father was busy making plans with the others for their escape. Now she was the sole witness as the window seal begin to bubble and warp. She screamed as the silicone seal twisted violently and the entire window fell out onto the sidewalk. It hit the concrete and the safety glass shattered into thousands of small pieces, yet remained intact. For the moment, it covered over the growing pool of sludge.

"We need to go now! Grab that fire extinguisher, Tucker." The sheriff grabbed Lana's arm and stepped up through the opening where the window had been. "Be careful. Don't get any of that shit on you!" he warned as he helped each one get through.

"Don't wait for me, just run to the trucks!"

# TWENTY ONE

The group dodged pools of black sludge as they ran for the trucks, two pickups and an SUV. The sheriff yelled to the others, "Like we planned, one man each in the pickups, everybody else in the SUV. Pile in that fucker! We are going out convoy style, the two pickups first. We'll plow a path through, and if the tires blow, abandon your trucks and get in the SUV. Who's driving?"

Two men raised their hands, and the sheriff pointed at one of them. "You drive the second truck." To the other, he said, "Give me the keys, I'm leading."

Everyone, except the sheriff and the other driver, piled into the SUV. While they fired up their engines, the sheriff rolled down his window and yelled back, "Let's go! Get behind me!'

He threw his truck in gear and turned toward the only street that could get them as far away as fast as possible. To his surprise, the first few blocks were clear. However, just at the edge of town, two dolls stood in the middle of the road. With a snake-like swerving motion, the sheriff maneuvered around them, and the others followed.

He didn't notice the music playing on the stereo as he focused out in front of the headlights, watching for anything that might be out in the road. *"Oh, we're halfway there..."* He was driving so fast, when he saw the group of inflatable dolls in his path, he ran right through them. *"Oh, oh, living on a prayer..."*

Instantly, the foul smell of the heinous fluid filled the cab as it splashed against the windshield. He could see the trucks behind him swerve to miss the mess he had made, but he couldn't see the road ahead. He turned on the windshield wipers to try to clear the glass. Almost immediately, the rubber wiper blades jumped to life. As the metal arms swished back and forth, the rubber tried to jump away from the glass. It sounded as though someone was banging on the windshield.

"Oh shit!" The sheriff switched off the wipers. Still unable to see clearly, he ran off the road and into a ditch, slamming into the bank of a built up driveway. The airbag in the steering wheel inflated and, a moment later, the front tires of the truck exploded. He sat stunned thinking he was hearing voices, when suddenly there was a white cloud of mist next to his door. Finally, he understood. Someone was yelling at him.

"Wait, don't get out yet!" It was Tucker hosing the truck down with the $CO^2$ extinguisher. Seconds later, he yelled, "Okay, come on!"

The sheriff opened the door, and the boy carefully helped him out, half dragging him to the SUV. Once there, the door was flung open and the boy shoved him into the back seat, slamming the door behind him. Tucker opened the front door, still clutching the fire extinguisher, and climbed into the lap of the man sitting there. "Go!"

The driver blew his horn, and the man driving the second truck pulled around the mess on the roadway and continued with the SUV in hot pursuit.

"That was a close one," the driver yelled over his shoulder. "We just might make it out of here alive."

"Thanks, Tucker. You saved my ass. I apologize for every bad thing I ever said about you. You're one hell of a kid and my daughter is a lucky girl to have a boyfriend like you."

"No problem, Sheriff Wilson."

Hope was short-lived when the driver of the lead truck hit the next group of dolls. He immediately lost control and crashed into a tree. The SUV continued past the mess on the road and stopped. Again, Tucker jumped out and ran to the truck with his fire extinguisher in hand. When he got to the wreck, he could hear the driver screaming and see him writhing behind the wheel.

The man threw open his door and tumbled out into the tall grass. Tucker jumped back as the man exploded. Flying pieces of gore narrowly missed the boy.

"Fucking hell!"

He tried to inspect himself in the glow of the headlights still lighting the woods beyond the tree. As he lowered the nozzle of the fire extinguisher, his attention was drawn toward the clouds. He heard something coming. It sounded like... jet engines! He dropped the canister and ran as fast as he could to the SUV.

"They're coming!"

Jumping through the open door, he nearly knocked the other man out of his seat. He slammed the door as the driver floored the truck. The boy tried to tell the others what was happening.

"I heard the jets, they're..."

A blinding light flashed from behind them. He turned to see Lana sitting in the back seat and reached his hand toward hers. Their fingers had barely touched when the shock wave from the blast washed over the truck, sending it tumbling end over end. It happened so quickly, there was no chance for anyone to scream. The fuel tank exploded as they rolled, and the truck and its occupants were engulfed by a wave of searing fire.

They were two miles from ground zero when the blast hit. It leveled and burned everything within a twenty-mile radius and fires were already spreading beyond its reach. Twenty-five thousand feet overhead, the roar of a jet signaled a confirmation pass to verify that the target had been destroyed.

"Operation Walker has been executed. We are returning to base."

The pilot switched off his radio and added, "Lord, forgive us." He crossed his heart with his gloved hand, made a wide turn and headed back to base, leaving the flaming wasteland of the town of Kensington behind.